JESUS CHRIST, M.B.A.

A GOSPEL FOR OUR TIMES

DONN WEINHOLTZ

Illustrated by
DAVID WEINHOLTZ

CONTENTS

MORGAN GOLDMAN

~

A nd so it came to pass in mid-September 2011, just off of Wall Street, the financial heart of the United States of America; Jesus, the son of Mary, a mild-mannered, young, financial manager appeared. Clad in a grey, three-piece suit, his hair to his shoulders, sporting a full beard, and his bare feet in leather sandals; he entered the headquarters of the giant investment bank, Morgan Goldman. Announcing his arrival to the receptionist, Jesus proclaimed,

"Hi, you can call me J.C. I'm here for my final interview."

"Yes, Mr. J.C., they are expecting you on the 14th floor. You may take the elevator."

Upon entering the office of the senior vice-president and shaking hands with its elegantly dressed occupant, J.C. took a seat directly across the expansive teak desk from the vice-president.

"So, J. C., since you've already had three interviews, and passed them with flying colors, I'll cut to the chase. What makes you think that you'll be a winner here at Morgan Goldman?"

"Well, in addition to being a self-starter and being willing to make extraordinary sacrifices, I have connections in **High** places."

"Super. It always helps to be well networked."

"Yeah, I think that I can bring in clients from around the entire globe."

"Great."

"And I display strong moral integrity."

"Hmmm, let's not get carried away, Son. After all, business is business. Now tell me, what problems, if any, do you think that you might encounter?"

Pausing to think, JC. carefully offered, "Well, I'm Jewish, so I might encounter antisemitism."

"You wouldn't be the first, My Boy."

"Yes, but I recently threw some money changers out of my temple, and the video went viral."

"I suppose that we can overlook a single indiscretion, as long as you promise not to do it again."

"Also, I expect to be crucified by the time that I'm in my mid-thirties."

"Not-to-worry, Kid. The media is brutal. They maul us all on a daily basis, but we always win in the end. Big Money has staying power."

After pouring himself a scotch on the rocks, and taking a swig, the vice-president leaned forward putting both hands on the desk and looking J.C squarely in the eye.

"I'm going to be frank with you, J.C. I have some reservations, based on your lack of Wall Street experience, but I think that you have promise, and I'm willing to take a chance on you. Welcome to Morgan Goldman, Son. I hope that your career here will be a long and lucrative one."

"Thank you, Sir, I am sure that my Father will be pleased."

"Glad to hear it, Lad. Now tell me a bit more about this father of yours. Who is he?"

"Well, he prefers to remain out of the spotlight, practically invisible. Let's just say that he manages a very large portfolio, and he is highly diversified. In fact, he has substantial interests everywhere on the planet. He has held them for a very long time."

Imagining a hedge fund manager, with ties to middle east oil, Silicon Valley, the aerospace industry, Japanese auto corporations, and more; the vice president couldn't control his glee.

"My God, this is a match made in Heaven! There's no telling how far you will be able to go with those kinds of connections and the strategic positioning that you will have here at Morgan Goldman. The sky is the limit !"

"I imagine that is a reasonable way to view it, Sir. I'm never quite sure of Father's plans, but I can assure you that he always comes out on top. He has his finger on the pulse of everything important."

"Sounds like my kind of guy."

"I hope so, Sir. I certainly hope so."

Several weeks later J.C. was standing in the middle of the Morgan Goldman office, surrounded by a group of his fellow workers, preaching.

"It is easier for a camel to pass through the eye of a needle than for a rich man to enter the Kingdom of Heaven."

Overhearing this blasphemy, the company's head of HRD whispered to the senior vice president who had okayed J.C's hire.

"Are you sure that we did the right thing hiring this guy? He's not sounding like a good fit."

"Not-to-worry. We're only using him in order to make a bundle off of his old man. I'll have a talk with him, and get him to reign in the idealism."

Later that day, back in the vice president's office.

"Now that you're fully on board, Kid, I'd like to hear your plans. What sort of clients are you going to line up? What are your overall investment priorities?"

"I'm so glad that you asked. I think that it will be great for everyone, a real win-win, if I can start feeding the hungry, maybe doing 5,000 a day, then adding more."

"Whoa, wait a minute, Sonny Boy! If that's what you're planning, you've landed in the wrong place. This is no bleeding- heart NGO."

"Oh, I know that. But capitalism has to evolve if it's going to survive. The handwriting is on the wall. You're the one who has to adjust your thinking, Sir. Let's just think of what I'm planning as **Prophet** sharing.

2

OCCUPY WALL STREET

~

A few days later, J.C. dropped in at the Occupy Wall Street encampment at Zuccotti Park, dressed in white shirt, tie and sandals. It didn't take long for a crowd to begin gathering around him. Standing on a park bench, he proclaimed:

"Do not lay up for yourselves treasures on earth..."

Two occupiers talked about what they were witnessing.

"This guy sounds like the real deal. Where'd he come from?"

"Nobody's quite sure, but the word on the street is that he was working at Morgan Goldman..."

"Oh, a One Per Cent infiltrator, maybe?"

"But they canned him after a few weeks."

"Oh, sweet!"

Meanwhile, J.C. continued preaching as the crowd grew:

"And forgive us our debts... especially those bad mortgages... And how about cutting us a break on those college loans...So the 99% who deserve it can inherit the earth."

Cheers went up throughout the crowd and reverberated down cavernous Wall Street. And J.C. continued:

"Woe unto the rich for they have already received their consolation..."

Upon hearing this, the first occupier turned to his friend and uttered:

"This sounds vaguely familiar. Where have I heard it before?"

To which his buddy responded:

"I don't know. Maybe Marx?"

"Groucho?'

"No, Karl."

Meanwhile on the 14th floor of the Morgan Goldman Building. The senior vice president and HRD head were looking down on J.C. and the burgeoning crowd surrounding him. The HRD head offered:

"It's a good thing that we fired that guy. Look at him down there, playing to the crowd. He's giving them what they want, and they're eating it up."

"Do you think that he is some sort of commie?

"Nah, more of a religious fanatic, a harmless shaman."

As they watched, J.C. was handed a bullhorn so the steadily growing masses could hear him.

"Be ye therefore merciful, as your Father also is merciful. Judge not, and ye shall not be judged: condemn not, and ye shall not be condemned: forgive, and ye shall be forgiven. Give, and it shall be given unto you….For with the same measure that ye mete withal, it shall be measured to you again."

Far above, looking wistfully out the window, the senior vice president thought:

"Too bad. What a waste. I kind of liked the kid."

But given the loud speaker system that J.C. now commanded the Morgan Goldman executives heard him as he bellowed:

"But I say unto you, love your enemies."

Which alarmed the senior vice president.

"Hey, he's crossing a line, sounding dangerous!"

"What do you mean?"

"For God sake, he's telling them to love us. It's so damned hard to foreclose on people claiming they love you!"

3

TAKE ME OUT TO THE BALLGAME

But JC stood up and waved his arms; first making the ball dance around, then causing it to rise up over the fence.

⁓

I n early October, 2011 the Yankees were playing the Detroit Tigers at home for the American League Eastern Division championship. J.C. sat in the right field bleachers, wearing a Tigers cap along with his vested suit and sandals, drawing merciless taunts from Yankee fans. In spite of the boo's, J.C. stood and scolded the fans:

"Shame on you. Blessed are the peacemakers for they will be known as the Children of God."

"What's with this dude?" yelled one disgruntled fan. "Where the hell did he come from?"

"I don't know," yelled another. "But with that hair and beard it looks like freakin' Johnny Damon is back, and he's gone over to the dark side. Booooooo!"

Seizing the opportunity for something dramatic, J.C. stood up in the stands, raising his arms above his head. As he did so, with bases loaded, the Yankees' Robinson Canó hit a routine fly ball to center field. Suddenly, the ball halted in mid-air, and as J.C. waved his arms, began dancing around. The stadium let out a collective gasp. Then, J.C. dropped his arms, the ball resumed its original trajectory, and passed over the fence for a grand slam. Bedlam erupted. The fans cheered wildly. J.C. climbed out of the stands, walked across the field and stood on second base, again raising his arms, to his now adoring fans.

Soon, two NYC police officers appeared and escorted J.C. off of the field. One asked:

"What's the deal buddy? You show up lookin' like Johnny Damon, impersonating Jesus Christ; work some hocus pocus on Canó's homer; then stand on second, getting yourself tossed. I mean, what the hell's going on?"

"Well, Officer, it's complicated. But can you think of a better way to announce a *Second Coming*?"

4

MAYOR MIKE

The next day's *New York Post* featured giant headlines, screaming "**Jesus Christ Impersonator Takes the Field.**"

J.C., meanwhile, woke up in jail. However, soon a group of his new followers posted bail, springing him from the clink. On his way out, a police sergeant ushering him to the door delivered an unexpected message:

"Hey, you've been summoned to the mayor's office. They said you should walk right in, and you'll get to meet with him."

"Thank you, Officer, I'll head right over. By the way, I've had a very pleasant visit. Many of the people staying with you have tremendous potential. I hope that you'll find ways to provide them with assistance, once their tenure here is over."

"Right, keep on dreamin', Buddy."

"I will, Officer. You can count on that, and I will be back, as I have previously said:

"I was in prison and you came to visit me ... I tell you the truth, whatever you did for one of the least of these brothers of mine, you did for me."

Upon arriving at the Mayor's office, J. C. was quickly escorted in.

"Hello, I'm J.C. You must be Mayor Bloomberg."

"Please, call me Mike. So, between your time at the Occupy encampment and your appearance at Yankee Stadium, you've developed quite a following."

"So it seems, Mike. But tell me about yourself. This is a huge, sprawling city. Are you the local equivalent to Pontius Pilate?"

"Well, I've never heard it put quite like that, but I imagine that there are parallels. I don't have the Roman army at my disposal, but our police force is large and well equipped. And I suppose that I make up for any further shortcomings by having a lot more money than he did."

"Yes, about all that money. I think that we could work quite well together."

"What do you have in mind?"

"I've noticed that many people in your city live in stark poverty, while others have opulent life-styles. I'd like you to set an example by giving your money away to the poor."

The mayor's eyes bulged and his draw dropped.

"Wait a minute. I give everything that I have to this city; my heart, my soul, my every waking hour."

"Your money?"

"Hey, give me a break. I make my fair share of donations. Have you read about Bloomberg Philanthropies?"

"Yes, very impressive, Mike, but you know that there is so much more that you can do, just in the area of health, alone."

"I'm working on that," said Bloomberg, who enthusiastically explained his initiative to eliminate extra-large soda cups at fast food restaurants to substantially reduce people's intake of junk calories.

"But, let's switch topics. Other than giving away all of my own money, as mayor, how can I help you?"

"I'm glad that you asked, Mike. I'm not ready to go public yet, but I'd really like your endorsement for my presidential campaign."

Mayor Mike's jaw dropped and his eyes bulged. Dumbfounded, he thought to himself.

"Wait a minute! I'm the one who should be running for president."

5

THE DAILY SHOW

~

Making his first, live, television appearance, J.C. joined Jon Stewart on *The Daily Show*. Jon started the discussion with a question.

"So what's a nice Jewish boy like you doing stirring up trouble in New York?"

"Heaven knows!

"How about giving me a straight answer?"

"I just did, Jon."

The audience broke up in laugher.

"Hmmm, you know that some people are starting to spread Messiah rumors."

"So I hear."

"How does that make you feel?"

"You might say that it's the *cross that I have to bear*."

More laughs followed.

"Others are saying that you might run for president."

"I can't rule it out, because it certainly is a way to get things done."

"What might stop you?

"Hmmm, maybe the birth certificate."

The audience erupted.

"So, what are you trying to accomplish?

"I hope to make capitalism subservient to the Golden Rule."

"It already is, J.C."

"How so, Jon?"

"The dudes with the most gold make all of the rules."

The audience responded with the biggest laughs of the night.

"That is funny, Jon; but seriously, we need an economy directed more by, *Do unto others, as you would have them do unto you*."

"Instead of?"

"Instead of, *Screw your brothers before they screw you*."

"Let's take a look at some other issues, J.C."

"OK, Jon."

"Where do you come down on the Catholic Church not wanting to pay for employee's birth control?'

"Well, in a world populated by over 7 billion people... We can't be relying on *immaculate contraception*."

The audience cracked up.

"What about renewable energy?"

"We will invest heavily in solar."

"Why?"

'Like I keep saying. *Trust in your Father and in the Sun*."

More laughs.

"What would you do with the military budget?"

"Cut it in half."

"That's a little extreme, isn't it?"

"The cure for this nation's defense is not to be so offensive."

"And who's providing you with guidance on defense issues?"

"Paul."

"As in Ron?"

"No, as in The Apostle."

The audience roared with laughter one last time, and Jon shook J.C.'s hand as the show came to a close. After a cursory goodbye offstage, Jon turned to his director.

"My God, book him as often as you can get him. He killed it, tonight. The guy's a natural."

25

6

THE EVENING NEWS

⮂

By mid-November, J.C. was receiving heavy news coverage, with television crews following him wherever he went. Upon coming out of the Eugene O'Neill Theater, after seeing the Book of Mormon, a TV reporter asked,

"J.C., what brought you out to see *The Book of Mormon.*

"I was hoping to learn more about the teachings of the prophet, Joseph Smith."

"What did you think of the show?"

"It was very funny, but it looks like I am still going to have to read the Book."

"While I have you here, do you have any thoughts about Mitt Romney being a Mormon?"

"I'm not sure that a candidate's religion makes much of a difference in a presidency."

"For example, Richard Nixon was raised a Quaker… and he carpet bombed North Vietnam."

One evening in mid-November, the weekend anchor of the evening news, Jack Flash, announced.

"In a fast-breaking story, within the last hour, the man who calls himself " J.C.", but who many are now calling "Jesus Christ M.B.A." walked out onto the frozen Hudson River and rescued a young girl who had fallen through the ice. With more on the story, here is our on-the-scene reporter, Kristen Steinway. What can you tell us, Kristen?"

"You've pretty much covered it , Jack, except for one thing."

"What's that, Kristen?"

"The river isn't frozen."

Flabbergasted, Flash spit out the logical question,

"Are you saying that he was walking on water?"

"According to about fifty witnesses, that's the way it appears, Jack."

"So how did he explain it, Kristen?"

"He didn't, Jack. When I asked him about how he did it, all he said was that he was happy to help, but he couldn't give away any family secrets."

"Can you get him on camera, so I can ask him a few questions, Kristen?"

"Sorry, Jack, he's left the scene. He said that he was going over to Mt. Sinai Hospital."

"Do you know why, Kristen?"

"He only said that, *It's time to start healing the sick*, Jack."

"Well, it sounds like you'll have to stay on top of his every move, Kristen. Stay tuned for more tonight on Eyewitness News at 11:00."

By the time the 11:00 news rolled around, Kristen had tracked down J.C.

"This is Kristen Steinway, standing in front of the emergency room entrance at Mt. Sinai Hospital, where the man known as Jesus Christ M.B.A. is laying hands on people before they can enter the hospital, declaring them cured, and sending them on their way. I'm going to try to get a statement from him."

Putting the microphone in front of J.C.'s face, Kristen asked:

"How long do you plan to keep this up, J.C.?"

"I'm not sure. How long do you think it will take this country to get a decent, single-payer health insurance system?"

Amused, but taken aback by the response, Kristen probed further,

"Is it true, as some people say, that you can also raise the dead?"

"I don't know. I haven't really tried."

"Well, if you could, who would you bring back to life?"

Pausing to reflect for a moment, J.C responded,

I'd probably resurrect Phil Donahue. I thought that his shows were great."

"But he's not dead," offered a perplexed Steinway.

"Maybe not, but Fox buried him in the ratings. I'd restore 30 years to his life and send him back into the ring."

7

THE O'REILLY FACTOR

~

The on-air discussion regarding Fox caused J.C. to think that perhaps he should accept the network's invitation for him to appear on the *O'Reilly Factor*. Within a week, he was on the show.

"So, what caused a pinko, Messiah impersonator like you to decide to relent and come on my show?"

"I thought you might provide me with the opportunity to practice what I preach, Bill."

"Such as?"

"Turn the other cheek."

"We'll see about that. Chicken-hearted liberal that you are, you must oppose the Military-Industrial-Complex. Right? What do you have to say for yourself?"

"Three little words, Bill."

"And they are?"

"I like Ike."

"Don't think that you can play that old Eisenhower Military Industrial Complex warning and get off easy."

"Do you have any idea how the safety of this country will be jeopardized by substantial cuts in our military forces."

"Yes, I do."

Looking smug, O'Reilly responded, "Tell me, Mr. Know-It-All, what will happen?"

"Since this is a military state, Bill, in a short time the economy will go into free fall. But the country will recover due to a rapid transition from military spending to focusing on developing a technology-driven economy capable of generating renewable resources, such as wind, solar and tidal energy, rather than remaining dependent on fossil fuels. It will finally be possible to invest in people's education and health the way that we should. A soundly-based peace and prosperity will flourish."

Looking appalled, O'Reilly muttered, "God help us."

"Believe me, Bill, I'm trying."

"O.K, Smart Ass, I can't take much more, but to show you what a *fair and balanced* guy I am, I'll give you the last word. Do you have anything else to say on your way out of here?"

"Thank you, Bill. That is very kind of you, and there is one more thing,"

"Spit it out."

"I'm pleased to announce, right here on your show, that I'm launching my candidacy for the presidency of the United States."

Shocked by the announcement, O'Reilly spoke up:

"Wait a minute. You're not getting out of here without doing some explaining, Buddy. We're holding you over for the next segment."

"That's fine with me, Bill. I'm so glad that you asked."

"We'll be back in a few minutes, friends, after a word from a few of our great sponsors."

After an array of commercials from, Lexus, Orkin, H&R Block and Subaru; the duo reappeared.

"So, you're going to have the audacity to challenge Barak Obama for the democratic nomination?"

"No, Bill. I don't identify with either of the corporate- dominated parties. I plan to run as an independent."

"Do you honestly think that you can generate the grass root support necessary to defeat both an incumbent Democrat and a well-funded Republican, whoever that might be?

"Bill, the Occupy Movement has shown that there is broad-based enthusiasm, among younger people in particular, for a new vision of what the world might be. Barak Obama has taken pragmatic steps in the right direction, but he and his party are still too beholden to the corporate power brokers to make vitally import change happen. I plan to be the person who breaks that strangle hold."

"You can't be serious."

"I couldn't be more serious, Bill. The poor are hurting, income inequality is out of control, the planet is increasingly sick and species are dying. This is no time for caution."

"It will take a miracle."

"Thank you. That sounds like it is right in my wheelhouse."

"I heard that you told Jon Stewart that you didn't even have a birth certificate."

"It was a joke Bill. I've got that covered."

"Oh yeah, where were you born?"

"Bethlehem."

"So, you're an alien, and probably illegal at that!"

"Pennsylvania!"

Pretty much *throwing down the mic* with that final announcement, J.C. stood up, waved to the T.V. audience and walked off the set.

8

THE CAMPAIGN

~

J.C. quickly developed a presidential campaign website, and recruited about 50 New York City "Occupiers" to staff his campaign headquarters. He was deluged with offers from other "Occupiers" from all 50 states offering to help him gather the necessary signatures and meet any other stipulations for him to fulfill each state's ballot requirements. If ever there was a "grass roots" campaign, this was it.

With small donations pouring in, J.C. was soon making appearances throughout the United States, traveling mostly by train, which he preferred because of its gentler environmental impact, compared to auto and air travel. He'd arrive in a city, take a bus or the subway to the local arena, speak to a packed house, then move on to the next location; sleeping and eating on the train.

At the Wells Fargo Center in Philadelphia, he rolled out his plans for demilitarization:

"Hello, Philly. I'm so glad to be here in the land of soft pretzels, Tastykakes, and cheese steaks."

The crowd roared its approval.

"I couldn't help but notice, during my train ride here today, how your beautiful city has large areas of urban blight butting up against gentrified neighborhoods, the historic sites and the spectacular new buildings of your Center City. It's time that we do more to support our urban poor by redirecting large sections of the bloated military budget into the creation of urban development zones. We can create new jobs focusing on sustainable energy generation. We just need the political will to do it. So, verily I say unto thee, Let's "GIT-R-DONE!""

A few days later, J.C. spoke about the farm economy, in Ames, Iowa at Iowa State's Hilton Coliseum,

"The Lord blessed Iowa with incredible soil, and your ability to provide the United States and the world with corn, soy beans, oats, flaxseed, rye and wheat is a great blessing. But many of you depend on mass producing hogs and cattle. My friends, this must change. Mother Earth can't support it. The dear animals consume too much feed and water and then pass too much methane. Since, as the Proverb tells us, 'the righteous care for the needs of their animals', we must lovingly tend to the existing livestock, while transitioning to plant-based meats. The soil will save us, but only if we save the soil."

And in Bozeman, Montana at Montana State's Worthington Arena, J.C. responded to questions about gun control.

"The Second Amendment is like a Rorschach Test. People see what they want to see. But I say unto you, it was inserted into the Constitution to ensure that the nation could raise a militia army of soldiers bearing flintlock rifles in order to protect a fledgling nation from invasion by the British or the French. The usefulness of this anachronistic law has passed. It must be repealed and sane gun control policies must be implemented. The reduction in suicides and homicides will be a great blessing upon the nation."

The crowd remained silent. Then a few boo's followed. J.C. was striking deep chords wherever he went, but not always positive.

Moving on to Seattle, J.C. addressed the packed Key Arena, tackling healthcare.

"We need only to look to the north to see a sane and humane health-care system. Canada takes care of its sick without casting them into devastating debt. The time for the foolishness of the current United States' healthcare system has ended. Under my administration, we will move to a single-payer approach, and that payer will be the United States government. President Obama, himself, has stated that 'if we could start from scratch' we would build a single-payer system like the nations of Europe did after World War II. Well, I say unto you, we will start over, go beyond Obama-care, and create an affordable healthcare system that lovingly provides care for every disease, all afflictions that plague our people, and any pandemic that awaits us. The needs of our entire population come before the needs of our insurance corporations!"

This time the message was embraced by a wildly cheering crowd. But in crossing the country and speaking his "truth," J.C. marked himself as the most controversial presidential candidate in U.S. history. And along with the throngs of supporters, were many fanatically opposed to his messages. Thousands of hate emails poured in to his campaign headquarters across the country.

"Go back to where you came from, you damned terrorist…"

"You want to tear down the greatest nation on earth. Go to Hell."

"Keep your hands off of my family doctor, you worthless piece of shit!"

"You stupid-ass vegan. You've got no idea what the fuck you're talkin' about!"

9

MARIA

~

Exhausted from his cross-country tour and the cumulative impact of all that had unfolded over the last few months, J.C. returned to New York and retreated to a small apartment, provided to him by a supporter, in the Fort Green section of Brooklyn. Evading reporters and paparazzi at Penn Central by wearing a hoodie and sunglasses, and catching an Uber immediately upon leaving the station; he settled into the apartment and slept for nearly 24 hours. Upon awaking, with a touch of his hand, he turned a glass of water into red wine and converted some leftover crusts of bread in the fridge into avocado toast and a veggie omelet. Then, after finishing his brunch - in jeans, ball cap, and hoodie –he went outside for a walk.

While strolling the crowded streets of Brooklyn, admiring the brownstones, trees and snarkly-dressed hipsters walking their dogs; J.C. came across a young, Latina woman, perhaps in her mid-twenties. She was sitting on the ground outside of a café, with her back to the wall, facing all who passed. Attractive, but shabbily dressed and unkempt, she held a sign in her lap saying, "I am homeless. Please help me." Others passed by, but J.C. went right to her, sat down next to her, and asked, "What is your name, and how might I help you?"

Much to his surprise, she stared lovingly in his eyes and said,

"My name is Maria. And you are the Son of God, aren't you."

"What makes you say that?"

"I've heard of your presence, and I knew that I would recognize you, if we ever met. So, the question is not, 'How can you help me?', but rather, 'How can I help you?'"

"Hmmmm, clearly we need to talk, but first, we need to get you something to eat. Let's go inside."

The café was crowded, as every decent café in Brooklyn is crowded in the early afternoon, but they found a table in the rear and settled in. After J.C. ordered Maria a substantial brunch and himself an herbal tea, Maria began explaining her plight, hungrily eating as she spoke.

"I came to New York three years ago from San Juan, Puerto Rico,

45

hoping to make it on Broadway; but from the start, nothing went right. My waitressing job didn't pay enough to meet my rent, so I had to take on roommates, two other struggling actresses. One of the girls had a cocaine habit, and when I got depressed, after so many near-miss auditions, I tried a little coke. Initially, I felt great, but the "highs" were never as good after the first few times. Soon, I was hooked, in even more serious financial trouble, and suffering from anxiety, insomnia, even deeper depression and headaches, so many headaches. Then, hoping to make a clean break and a fresh start, I moved in with a guy, Damien, who had a good job in finance and a nice apartment in Manhattan. He was sweet at first, but soon he showed his dark side. He'd yell at me for not keeping the apartment clean and having dinner ready for him. It was crazy because I was still waitressing and auditioning. I couldn't be a housewife. Getting desperate and anxious, I started snorting coke again, and then he started hitting me. The whole situation just got worse and worse. I couldn't take it anymore, and a couple of months ago, I packed up some clothing and bailed. I came to Brooklyn to avoid Damien, and I've been on the streets, and in and out of shelters, ever since."

J.C. listened intently, and as he did Maria, noticed herself feeling stronger and more confident than she had for a long time. J.C. spoke.

"You'll not have to worry about the cocaine addiction any longer. I've taken care of that."

"How? How can you possibly...?"

"You, more than anyone I have met, know who I am, and you still ask?"

"Of course, you are right. Thank you, so much. I am blessed. You've saved my life. What can I possibly do to repay you?"

"Well, here is the awkward part. I have chosen not to have a group of disciples surrounding me. There really is no need any longer for such a group. Word spreads so quickly in the modern era, and the Occupiers are so willing to assist me in all of my work."

"So what is the awkward part?"

"Well, you have been chosen."

"Chosen?"

"Yes, chosen."

"For what?"

"To be my companion."

"WHAT?"

"I told you it would be awkward."

"What does it mean?"

"It means that you will move in with me and accompany me wherever I go. You will be my confidante. This work isn't easy. I need somebody to talk to, and you are that person. My Father told me that your identity would be revealed to me at the proper time, and that time has come. You are the one."

"How can you be sure?"

"Maria, believe me, I know these things; and you know why I know them."

"Yes, I do. But this has all happened so fast. I wasn't expecting this. Going from the worst possible situation, barely existing living on the streets, to this in one afternoon is a breathtaking change."

"Yes, it is, but I can assure you this. You will be rewarded beyond all of your expectations, and you won't have to do it for very long."

"Why is that?"

"Because I won't be here that much longer. There are people who find me threatening. I don't know exactly when, but they will eliminate me. However, my messages will live on, and you will help to maintain and spread them."

And from that moment on they were inseparable. From the café, they went to the Brooklyn Flea Market to buy Maria some clothing. Then they returned to the apartment so she could shower and rest. When she awoke, J.C. laid out his strategy for the remainder of the presidential campaign.

THE UNITED NATIONS

Following his coupling with Maria, the first major event on J.C.'s schedule, was a speech to the U.N. General Assembly; requested by Secretary General Ban Ki-moon. Ban asked J.C. to focus on the state of the planet; so he addressed climate change and the overall degradation of the environment.

"It is my great privilege to be with you today. Looking out at this sea of beautiful faces representing the nations of the world, I am humbled and honored. But I am also aware of my sacred responsibility to speak the truth to you about the dire consequences confronting you as the result of human overpopulation, fossil fuel dependency, run-away industrialization, corporate-intensive farming, the wasting and spoiling of precious water, over-fishing, rampant resource depletion, and toxic chemical dispersion. As the *Old Testament* prophets pleaded with the people of Israel to honor their covenant with God, I plead with you today to respect and preserve our Mother Earth"

J.C. spoke for over an hour to the assembled delegates, meticulously warning them, in the most dire terms, of the consequences facing them and future generations if immediate, drastic actions were not implemented. In particular, he laid the burden of responsibility for change on the most powerful nations.

"And I say to you, the leaders and people of the United States, the European Union, China, India, Brazil, the oil-rich Arab states and Russia; the burden lies predominantly on you for reversing the tragic course that humanity has relentlessly pursued. You are the great consumers of goods and resources, as well as the dominant polluters. It is time for a world-wide pact among nations establishing a broad array of climate and environment actions; and the most developed nations must lead the way and must make the greatest sacrifices."

Predictably, the delegates from the world's struggling, developing nations cheered J.C.; standing and interrupting his talk with applause and shouts of approval, throughout. Meanwhile, those from the wealthy nations remained seated and quiet. They did not take kindly to this sort of scolding, but JC pressed on.

"Dear Capitalists, everywhere, as the Native American, Cree prophet taught us, *When all the trees have been cut down, when all the animals have been hunted, when all the waters are polluted, when all the air is unsafe to breathe; only then will you discover you cannot eat money.*"

Upon leaving the U.N., J.C. and Maria were immediately surrounded by TV, radio and newspaper reporters asking J.C. how he thought his dressing down of the developed countries had been received.

"It was deeply appreciated by those who shall inherit the earth, but not by those who shall have great difficulty entering the kingdom of heaven."

"Do you think that your warnings will make a difference?"

"Not immediately. Frankly, things will probably have to get much worse before necessary, radical actions are taken; and by then it may be too late. Fortunately, there are compelling prophets who are already out there trumpeting these vital messages."

"Who?"

"In North America, Bill McKibben, Paul Watson, and Al Gore immediately come to mind, as do Winona LaDuke and Julia Butterfly Hill."

Elsewhere around the world, there are many distinctive voices, especially females such as India's Vandana Shiva, Australia's Aila Keto and Brazil's Marina Silva. In spite of her recent death, Wangari Maathai's work, planting 30 million trees and fighting for social justice in Kenya, has inspired so many activists. The torch will be passed from generation to generation. In fact, she doesn't even know it yet, but young girl named Greta is out there in Sweden being groomed by events around her. When she finally awakens to her calling, she will make an impact unlike any before her. And because solutions will ultimately be political, a new generation of politicians will have to respond to the call. Right here in New York, a young woman named Alexandria will appear with a vision of a New Deal for the environment. Others must follow."

"Ok, and speaking of women, who is the lovely young woman who has been accompanying you everywhere during the last few weeks?"

"This is my dear friend, Maria. If you have any questions about her, you'll have to ask her directly. She speaks for herself."

"So, Maria, what do you have to tell us about yourself?"

"No comment, for now; but I assure you, we'll be talking a lot, soon."

11

THE MOB

~

Over the next several weeks, J.C. and Maria traveled constantly around the country making campaign appearances. Because he was not affiliated with any party, he did not have to worry about winning any primary campaigns or caucuses, giving him a leg up on Republicans, who were tied up in Iowa, New Hampshire and South Carolina. On the other hand, the Democratic nomination was already sewn up by President Obama, who J.C. knew would be his most formidable opponent in a three-way race. J.C. was personally fond of Obama and his family, but he knew that the capitalist machinery in the United States would only let Obama accomplish modest incremental changes. J.C. had been sent to emphasize the urgency of the problems confronting the nation and the planet, and he would press the message relentlessly.

Meanwhile, in a back room in a northern New Jersey restaurant, dark forces were formulating alternative plans for J.C.'s future. The heads of two mob clans discussed their dilemma.

"This guy is leading a revolution. He's got to go down."

"Yeah, he's bad for business. It's taken a long time for us to set up companies with huge government contracts. We can't have him gettin' in there and pokin' around. How do you want to move on him."

"Well, bribes aren't gonna work. And he'll probably just call us out on any death threats. We gotta erase him."

"How about a joint effort, your guys and mine?"

"Sounds good."

"When?"

"The sooner the better."

"Ok, as soon as he comes back to the city. We'll make the hit."

Arriving back in New York after campaign stops in Albany, Hartford, Boston and New Haven; J.C. and Maria decided that they needed some down time, and they retreated to the apartment in Brooklyn. Although they were pretty much under 24-hour news reporter and paparazzi surveillance, J.C., attired in his hoodie, could sneak out the basement fire exit at the back of his building, and evade the throngs via the alley.

On their second evening back, Maria fell asleep around 11:30 PM; but feeling restless, J.C. decided that he needed to get out for a walk, down by the river. Making his way out the back of the building, he snuck down the alley to Flatbush Avenue, then headed west towards the Brooklyn Bridge. Upon reaching the waterfront, he began strolling along the river with the Manhattan skyline to his right and Brooklyn to his left. Deep in thought, J.C. did not notice the black SUV with tinted windows that pulled up slowly behind him.

Suddenly, when no other cars or pedestrians were in sight, three mobsters leaped out of the car, while the get-a-way man remained behind the wheel. In no time at all, they were on top of J.C., pummeling him into submission, and wrapping him in chains.

One of the mobsters taunted him,

"Get ready to meet your maker, God Man."

Another added,

"Yeah, Jesus Freak, the end is near."

J.C. calmly responded,

"Forgive them, Father, they are so clueless!"

Once J.C. was chained and unconscious, they pulled a large safe from the back of the SUV, shoved J.C. inside, locked the door shut, and pushed the safe into the river.

"Have fun savin' the fishies Mr. Messiah!" said one mobster.

"Turn out the lights, the party's over," sang another.

"Oh my God! What have we done?" thought the third.

The whole operation only took a few short minutes; but as the safe headed to the bottom of the East River, a bolt of lightning struck near them and a deafening thunder clap shook the entire area. Terrified, the mobsters jumped into the SUV, and burned rubber out of there. The four were so startled that they didn't notice that a lone bicyclist had been approaching as they were finishing off J.C. They were gone by the time that he reached the crime scene, but he had witnessed the murder and had pulled out his cell phone and called 911.

"Hello, Operator, I think…I think…that I've just seen someone killed

59

down by the river, right near the Brooklyn Bridge, on the Brooklyn side."

Within minutes, two police cars arrived.

"So, what did you see, Sir?" asked the first officer.

"There were three of them, and they were beating this man. I'm not sure, but I think that it's the guy who's been all over the TV lately. You know, the one who is running for president."

"You mean J.C."

"Yeah, I think it was him."

"Did he resist?" asked the second officer.

"That's the funny thing. I don't think that he put up any kind of fight at all. In fact, as I was getting closer, I think I heard him say, 'I love you, and I forgive you.' It was freaky. Anyway, they had him wrapped up in chains and they pushed him into a safe, which they dropped into the river. It should be down there on the bottom, right below us."

"Did you get the license plate on the vehicle?" asked the first officer.

"No, I'm pretty sure that they were Jersey plates, but I didn't make out the numbers. It know it was a black SUV, I think a BMW.

It all happened so fast, and then the lightning and thunder hit. It was freakin' scary. I'm really shaken up."

"That's completely understandable, Sir. You've been through a lot." Said officer number two. "Still, we'd like you to stay with us, while we get a crane down here and pull that safe out of the water."

"Sure, Officer."

It took over an hour for the small crane to arrive, along with two police divers to attach cables around the safe so it could be hoisted to the surface. As the safe was being pulled up, the first officer commented out loud,

"This is not gonna be pretty."

When the safe was stable on the ground, the police locksmith started working on the combination lock. Meanwhile, a mobile television news crew arrived and started reporting.

"This is Kristin Steinway reporting from the bank of the East River close to the Brooklyn Bridge. Police are about to open a safe just pulled from the river that allegedly contains the body of the presidential candidate who people are calling *Jesus Christ M.B.A."*

The locksmith finally broke the combination. The door swung open.

"Where's the body?" somebody shouted.

"There is no body," yelled another.

"What's in there?" asked the first police officer.

"Just this note, in magic marker, on a handkerchief," responded the second officer.

"What's it say?"

"To Be Continued in 2000 Years."

Standing there aghast, the bicyclist cried out,

"But I swear that he was in there. I swear to God."

AFTERWARDS

S ometime around 3:00 AM, Maria awoke and wandered into the apartment living room where she found J.C. sitting in a chair, soaking wet.

"Hi, why are you up in the middle of the night? And why are you so wet?"

"I'm no longer of this world, Maria."

"What do you mean?"

"It's time for me to go home. In fact, I already left and I've come back. I wanted to say goodbye, and to make sure you understand what is going to be expected of you."

"Yes, I think that we'd better get that straight."

And so, they talked throughout the remainder of the night, with J.C. explaining how Maria would have to carry his messages of caring for each other and caring for the earth to the far corners of the planet. He told Maria that she would have to be prepared for endless media appearances and much travel, but that she wouldn't have to worry. She would always be protected and provided for. She could lead a fearless life.

Then at dawn, he kissed her on the forehead and bid her farewell, telling her that he had one remaining stop to make before ascending to home.

"Where will you be going?

"To Zuccotti Park, where all of this began. I want to bid farewell to the Occupiers and to bless them for their holy efforts."

Suddenly he vanished. Maria never saw him again.

In the early morning sky above Zuccotti Park, J.C. hovered for several minutes looking lovingly on the encampment below. A few early risers claim to have seen him and to have heard him saying:

"Blessed are those who hunger and thirst for righteousness, for they will be filled.

Blessed are the merciful, for they will be shown mercy.

Blessed are the pure in heart, for they will see God.

Blessed are the peacemakers, for they will be called children of God."

Dumbfounded by what they were witnessing, none the handful of Occupiers who saw J.C. recorded him on their phones. To this day, there is no record of his appearance other than their astonished reports. However, the video of the empty safe hauled out of the Hudson River went viral, producing billions of hits around the world.

Nevertheless, since the four, assassin mobsters were never found, the claims of the bicycling witness were the only "proof" of the miracle. These were dismissed by most.

For a few weeks, J.C.'s disappearance was the biggest media story in the world, but soon the sheer weight of the daily, 24-hour, news cycle buried J.C. in a way that the mob couldn't. The U.S. election (absent J.C.), the Benghazi attack, the conclusion of the Sandusky trial, Super Storm Sandy, the Newtown shooting, the escalating tragedy of the war in Syria, and so many other events moved J.C. to fringe status on the internet. He became a new 21st century cult figure adored by a large, but marginal, number of true believers. Along with the Occupy movement, J.C. and his timeless, powerful messages faded from public consciousness.

Meanwhile, Barack Obama was reelected. He did his best to steer the gargantuan, capitalist nation to a more humane course; advocating for sane gun control, pushing for vital environmental policies, protecting the Dreamers, supporting gay rights, and increasing health-care coverage. However, his domestic efforts were largely stymied by a stubbornly obstructionist Republican party. And in his foreign policy, he became increasingly accepting of civilian "collateral damage" resulting from drone warfare designed to deploy massive U.S. military force, while minimizing U.S. Middle East casualties. Although the economy steadily improved, the nation became increasingly polarized, and darker forces coalesced within the nation's right wing.

By 2016, the era of Donald Trump was upon the nation. In moments of despair, those who remembered J.C. and many others could only look to the sky and plead,

"Heaven Help Us!"

13

DIGITAL STRIPS

To view the illustrations as digital strips on the web, please visit:

https://donnweinholtz.com/jcmba

www.ingramcontent.com/pod-product-compliance
Lightning Source LLC
Chambersburg PA
CBHW070353130626
46556CB00007B/3151